ωS

The Voyage of the Silver Bream

For Jean and Lee

The Voyage
of the
Silver Bream

Theresa Tomlinson

A & C Black • London

VICTORIAN FLASHBACKS

Soldier's Son • Garry Kilworth
A Slip in Time • Maggie Pearson
Out of the Shadow • Margaret Nash
The Voyage of the Silver Bream • Theresa Tomlinson

also available:

WORLD WAR II FLASHBACKS

The Right Moment • David Belbin
Final Victory • Herbie Brennan
Blitz Boys • Linda Newbery
Blood and Ice • Neil Tonge

First paperback edition 2002
First published 2001 in hardback by
A & C Black (Publishers) Ltd
37 Soho Square, London, W1D 3QZ

Text copyright © 2001 Theresa Tomlinson
Cover illustration copyright © 2001 Mike Adams

ISBN 0-7136-5852-5

A CIP catalogue record for this book is available
from the British Library.

Printed and bound in Great Britain by
Creative Print & Design (Wales), Ebbw Vale.

Contents

Map of the Sheffield and South Yorkshire Waterway

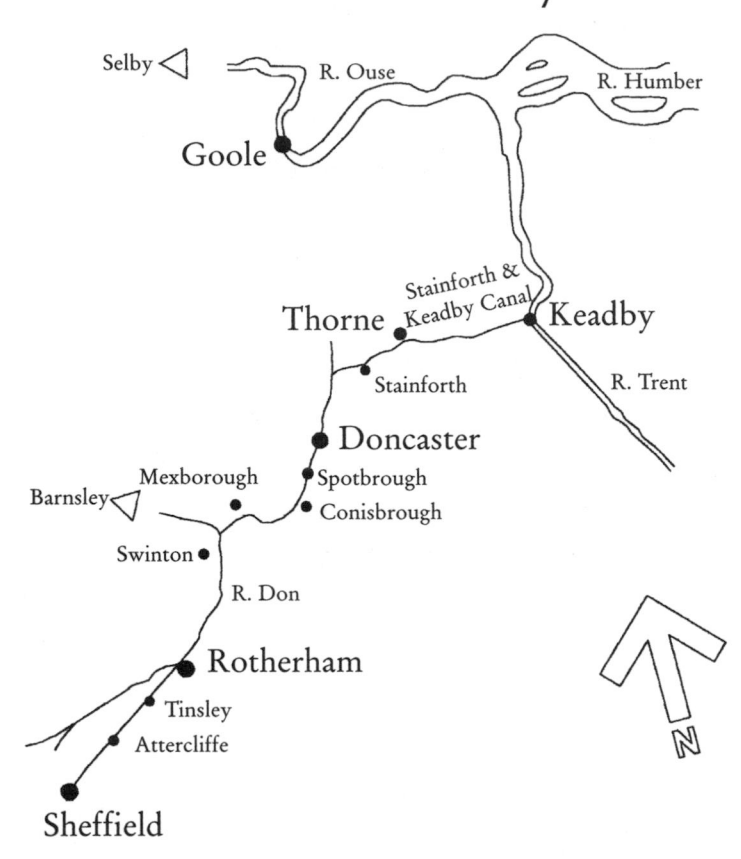

Distance from Sheffield Canal Basin along waterway to Keadby approximately 43 miles. From Keadby to the River Humber about another 10 miles.

Author's Note

The Sheffield to Tinsley Canal was opened in 1819, with great celebration. A crowd of 60,000 gathered in the Canal Basin where a cannon was fired and a brass band played, followed by food and drink in the local pubs. This was the first time that boats had ever been able to reach Sheffield. A navigable waterway now stretched from Sheffield, via Rotherham, Doncaster and Keadby, right down to the River Humber, linking Sheffield with Kingston-upon-Hull and from there, the rest of the world. Bulky items of iron, coal, timber and grain could now be transported into Sheffield Canal basin by water, while finished steel, cutlery and tools could be carried away by boat.

The building of the canal had first been suggested 120 years earlier, but it had been opposed by mill-owners along the River Don, who were concerned that their source of water power would be interfered with. Successive Dukes of Norfolk used their considerable influence in parliament to oppose the canal, as they owned many of the mills and were also concerned that the opening of the canal would make cheap coal from South Yorkshire more accessible, rivalling their own coal company.

So despite the enthusiastic celebrations, the opening of a waterway to Sheffield came rather late. The waterway experienced a short period of prosperity, but this lasted for only about twenty years. Once railways began to be built, canal and river transport began to suffer. The railways took away a great deal of traffic from the waterways, carrying goods faster, though they were never able to move the huge, heavy loads that the waterways could manage. It is at this time of rivalry and struggle that my story is set.

The Yorkshire boats were known as keels and they were much broader than a 'narrowboat'. They had a round-ended fore and aft, with a mast and two square sails that could be lifted on and off. The sails were used in the lower stretches of the waterway and the River Humber, but wherever a sail could not be used, a horse would haul the boat. Owner-captains often worked alongside their wives and children, and boat families would spend a lot of time aboard the keel, travelling from place to place. It was a hard life and the people must have been tough; they were often known for their 'rugged' language! When they faced difficult times they would cut costs by dispensing with the horse and bow-hauling the boat themselves.

It is just such a family that appear in the story, facing their own particular crisis. All the characters are fictitious, but I have tried to make their lives resemble those of the real boat families as closely as I could.

I would like to acknowledge the help and advice of Mike Taylor, author of several books on the Sheffield and South Yorkshire waterway. Also Martin Heywood, whose historical canal trips from Sheffield Canal Basin made a starting point for this book.

1 ❖ The Cottage by the Canal

1853

I stood on the towpath, that sunny afternoon in July. I was enjoying a holiday from school and staring up the canal towards Stainforth. I was waiting for the first glimpse of our Sheffield-sized keelboat – the *Silver Bream*. Mam had sent me as lookout, for Dad was expected and she was preparing a fine mutton stew for him and Tommy, who worked as his mate.

Izzie, my eight-year old sister, came running down the cottage path towards me. 'Jack!' she called. 'Mam's in a right fuss; she says t'stew will be spoilt. They should a' been here at noon.'

'Well it's no good squawking at me!' I told her. 'There's nowt I can do; there's no sign o' them!'

'Does tha think summat's wrong?' she asked, her eyes wide and worried.

I shrugged my shoulders. 'I wish I were with 'em instead o' standing here watching all the boats go by. One day I'll go with 'em and I'll sail right down to the sea!'

'Oh, will you?' said Izzie, not really interested in my plans. 'Well – I'm starving and Mam won't let me eat till Dad's back.'

She took a step closer to the water's edge and I came up behind her, pretending to push her in, though I really held onto her very tight. 'Neeps'll get thee!'

'No they'll not,' she yelled back. 'Neeps is lucky!'

'Not if you make 'em cross,' I teased.

Izzie believed firmly in the water sprites that we called Neeps, who were supposed to live in the River Don. Neeps could be wicked or kind, depending on whether they took a fancy to you or not.

I let Izzie go and we both turned and wandered back up the path to our small cottage that stood by the cut, on the outskirts of Stainforth. We lived in a little house almost surrounded by water, with the Stainforth and Keadby Canal in front and the River Don behind.

It was warm and cosy inside the cottage. Tansy, our old tabby cat, snoozed on the sunny windowsill. The big pan of stew bubbling away on the stove smelled delicious, while Mam busied herself bringing dry washing in from outside.

'Now then, Jack. Is there still no sign o' them yet?'

I shook my head. 'There's three keels gone by loaded wi' grain, but none o' them's the *Silver Bream*.'

Mam clicked her tongue, shaking her head. 'Where've they got to? Get back outside Jack, and shout 'em to hurry, as soon as tha catches sight o' them.'

I began to walk down to the cut again, shading my eyes from the sun so that I could see better. Another broad-built keel was being hauled steadily down the waterway towards us by a plodding horse. Suddenly I stopped, for I could see that Dad's mate Tommy had stepped ashore from it and was walking down the towpath towards me.

I turned then and ran back to Mam. 'Tommy's here! He's just stepped off the *Sweet Sarah*, but there's still no sign o' Dad.'

Mam frowned, looking puzzled. Dad paid Tommy to help him take the *Silver Bream* up and down the waterway, from the Humber to Sheffield Canal Basin and back again. Tommy came from Sheffield, and though he was getting old now and not so steady on his legs, still Father said that he was more reliable than many who were younger and fitter.

'What's he doing here, ahead of Alfie?' Mam wondered. But Tommy followed me in through our doorway and when we saw his face, we knew at once that something was wrong.

'An accident?' Mam breathed.

'Nay,' Tommy spoke up at once to reassure her. 'Not to thy man anyway. It's Jasper, your poor old horse – he's in the knacker's yard.'

'What?' I cried. 'Jasper? Dead?'

Izzie burst into tears. 'No!' she sobbed.

Jasper had been with us ever since I could remember. He was the sturdy black horse who patiently pulled our keelboat, leaning steadily into the rope. Jasper always managed to get the *Silver Bream* to move, however loaded up she might be.

'But he was fine when you set off! What happened to him?' I cried.

'Aye, a grand horse, Jasper, but getting old like me,' Tommy sighed. 'Truth to tell, he's been shaky of late and now the poor fellow's dead. Don't take on so, sweetheart.' He patted Izzie on the head. 'I think it was his heart that gave up. He stumbled into the water and by the time we managed to get him out, he'd drowned.'

'Could Father do nowt?' Izzie demanded.

Tommy shook his head. 'Even Alfie couldn't help him.'

My father, Alfie North, was the best horseman on the waterway, and I knew that if anyone could have saved Jasper it would have been him. Dad was always being asked to help out with other folks' horses.

'Now, tha knows he'd a' done his best.'

Izzie knuckled the tears away and nodded her head.

All this time Mam had watched us in worried silence, her mouth open, but saying nothing, when I'd have expected her to be plying Tommy with questions. I realised, with a nasty touch of sickness in my stomach, that there might be more to this than our horse being dead, though that was bad enough.

Tommy pulled a handful of coins from his pocket. 'Paid off,' he shook his head. 'Your dad has paid me off!'

'No,' I couldn't believe it. 'Not thee, Tommy. He'd never get rid o' thee!'

But Mam didn't seem very surprised. She shook her head, 'I'm so sorry, Tommy,' she said. 'So this is it – we've come to the end.'

'Aye missus,' Tommy swallowed hard.

'End o' what?' I demanded.

'I'm sorry, Jack,' Tommy said. 'It's the end o' the *Silver Bream*; leastways for us it is. We've been struggling ever since that damned railway line opened,' he spat. 'We can't compete with 'em. We've had to lower our prices, down and down again, so that we make no profit at all and now losing Jasper... well that's it! It's finished us!'

I nodded and I did understand; we'd all heard Father's complaints. Even before the railway line was built, the boatmen had been forced to lower their rates of carriage. They'd done it first to try to dissuade the railway companies from building their lines near the canal, and for a while that had worked. But as time went by, more railways were built and at last a line was set up from Doncaster to Swinton so that goods could now be carried by rail right up into Sheffield. Since then all the boatmen had been struggling to make ends meet. It was worst of all for keel captains like our dad, who worked their one boat, up and down the waterway.

'Tha father won't have the price of a new horse,' Mam said, her voice full of despair. 'And he won't have cash left to hire help; I knew well enough, that an accident such as this could finish us off.'

'Aye, that's the top and bottom of it, missus,'

Tommy agreed. 'Alfie's stuck up at Rotherham with a load o' grain.'

'So what's he going to do?' Mam asked.

'He'll try to get the loan of a horse to get the grain delivered, but then he says to tell thee that he's selling the *Silver Bream*. Mind you, it'll be tricky with the mast and leeboards left down at Wike Well Bridge.'

Keels like the *Silver Bream* could be sailed on the lower stretches of the waterway, but once they got to Thorne they had to leave the mast and sails ashore and travel on with a horse to pull the boat.

'Alfie says he'll come back here to see thee,' said Tommy, 'before he goes off looking for work as a navvy.'

'What?' I cried. I couldn't believe it. 'He'd never go digging tracks for the damned railway company; them that's done us in! Not my dad!'

2 ❖ Beggars Can't be Choosers

Mam looked very upset and I wished at once that I'd not spoken quite so sharply. 'It's a case of 'beggars can't be choosers',' she said, her voice breaking with distress.

'He could get work as a captain's mate,' Tommy said. 'But when you've owned your own keel, and you'd see it going up and down the cut in someone else's hands, well…?'

I nodded, guessing how bad that would feel.

Mam sat down with a bit of a jolt and put her head down into her hands. Izzie ran to stroke her hair. 'Don't fret, Mam,' she whispered.

I went to comfort her too then. 'It'll be all right,' I soothed, though I couldn't think how.

'Tha father's a good man,' Tommy spoke with respect. 'He's paid me all he owes; nobody could have been fairer. He's the best captain I've ever worked for and it grieves me sore that it comes to this.'

I stood in silence over Mam, stroking her back, but deep inside me anger grew, making me want to burst out shouting and fighting.

'I can't believe it's come to this,' Tommy shook his head. 'I was one of them that built that cut, up at Sheffield. I'd been away fighting old Bonaparte and Sheffield Town was full of men like me, back from the wars and swarming through the streets with no way to earn our bread. Then they had this clever idea – "Let's build that canal we always promised oursens and fetch the waterway from the River Don at Tinsley, right up into Sheffield. We can set all these hungry chaps to work on it." It were a grand idea.'

'Of course it was,' Mam answered him gently, lifting her head again.

'But it were hard work though! Cutting our way through solid rock wi' nowt but picks and shovels. I swore then that I'd work on the canal when it were finished, and I did. You should've seen the crowd that filled Sheffield Basin on the day they opened it – they went wild. They fired off cannons and a brass band played. The masons and the sick clubs paraded with fancy banners while everyone cheered.'

Mam smiled sadly. 'I were only a young lass, but all the boatmen's families went up there for it too; it were a day I'll never forget.'

Tommy's voice grew soft as he remembered.

'We'd never seen anything like that cut coming into town – a great water road, bearing coal and grain, all steady and silent-like; heavy loaded keels, that passed through fields and pastures.'

We'd heard all this before from Old Tommy, but we'd never really listened properly. Suddenly his story seemed to be full of sadness and importance.

'Now, they say it's old-fashioned and slow,' he continued. 'And it is,' he nodded his head. 'Compared to these trucks that run on iron rails, it is, but I tell you this; those little trucks can't take the great heavy bulk that our keels can. They'll find that out. They'll find that out, but it'll maybe be too late by then.'

We were quiet for a while, but then Mam seemed to gather herself together and remember her manners. 'We've a mutton stew to offer thee, Tommy.'

But Tommy shook his head. 'I'll be on my way,' he said. 'I'll try to get myself taken on down at Wike Well and the sooner I'm there, the sooner I'll be working again. I just promised Alfie I'd let thee know what's up! I don't like to be the bearer of bad news, not one bit!'

We all went outside with him and walked down to the gate. My knees were like jelly and my stomach churned. I couldn't believe it: just thirty minutes ago our lives had seemed so cosy and comfortable, now everything had changed. I'd heard about men going off to work as navvies, and hardly seeing their families. They had a terrible time of it, working day and night away from home and they were known for rough ways and fighting. Frank Woodall's father had gone off to help dig a great tunnel and he'd been killed; crushed beneath a fall of rocks. I hated to think of Father leaving the waterway to do a job like that.

We stood quietly by our gatepost, watching Tommy limp off up the towpath towards Wike Well. Then Izzie spoke and I knew that she'd been thinking the same as me. 'I'm scared,' she whispered. 'Scared our dad might get crushed in a tunnel, like Frank's did.'

Mam put an arm about each of us. 'I've feared this coming a long time,' she said. 'I don't want tha father working as a navvy either, but truth to tell there's no job that I can think of that keeps a man safe. If they work in the mines there's danger, if they're making steel, it's the same. Tha father's a sensible man and if anyone can keep himself safe he will.'

We drifted back to the cottage, still shocked by

Tommy's news. Mam had taken the stew off the stove, but none of us had much of an appetite now.

'We should eat,' Mam told us without enthusiasm, but after a few mouthfuls I threw down my spoon.

'The damned railways,' I shouted. 'It's just not fair! I'd blast 'em all to hell, I would!'

'I'll have none o' that language here!' Mam snapped at me. Then she sighed and patted my arm. 'I'm vexed as you are Jack; all these years that your father's worked so hard. We thought that if he kept going and stuck at it, we'd see this difficult time through.'

'There's gotta be something we can do,' I insisted. 'I could go down Hatfield Pit. I'm old enough now.'

'You're not doing that!' Mam answered back at once, as I knew she would – and I also knew she meant it. No one spoke, while she tapped her fingers on the table, irritated and thoughtful.

Terrible pictures filled my head. How could we sell the *Silver Bream*? How could we watch our keel passing up and down the cut belonging to one of the bigger companies? I loved the broad-built Yorkshire keel that had earned our bread ever since I could remember. The waterway was all that Father knew about… it was all that any of us knew.

Mam gave a sudden snort that made us jump; she slapped her hand down sharply on the table, then sat up very straight and determined looking. 'There is another way!' she said.

'What? What?' we both cried.

'Others have always done it! Peggy Moxon was telling me last week that they're all at it in Manchester now. Whole families of 'em, rough as monkeys, swarming all over the decks. And there's always been some of the Stainforth chaps that go up to Sheffield with their missus as mate.'

Izzie and I looked at each other, suddenly hopeful. This was a very big change of heart for Mam. She'd always insisted that we were not to start living on the *Silver Bream*. She looked down her nose a little at those families who worked aboard their boat, telling us tales of rats biting babies, terrible drunkenness and battles at every lock.

'We three could go up to Rotherham,' Mam said now. 'We'd help your father take that load o' grain up to the Canal Basin oursens. I'd act as mate and Jack, tha'd open and close the lock gates and Izzie too. If we did all right we could start to take the

Bream up and down the waterway ourselves, with no extra wages to pay!'

'Yes!' we cried.

3 ❖ Better Than Going Down a Mine

Though we were cheered at the thought of going to work on the *Silver Bream*, Mam still looked grim. 'I hate the idea,' she said through gritted teeth. 'But… it would be better than having my man away navvying or my son down a mine!'

'Oh yes!' Izzie and I both agreed.

Then suddenly Mam's enthusiasm vanished and her face crumpled.

'What is it?' I asked. 'It's a grand idea and we're right willing.'

Her voice went very small and childlike. 'No horse,' she whispered. 'No horse.'

My heart sank worse than before at that. Mam had suggested what we'd never have dared, but now the despairing silence had come back and I couldn't bear it. Anything was better than that.

'If we could just manage to get this load delivered,' I said. 'Then maybe we could hire a horse.'

Mam looked up at me, frowning and thoughtful. 'There's always – bow-hauling – I suppose,' I spoke the words reluctantly.

'Bow-hauling? Thee?' Izzie was amazed and she'd every right to be. They both knew how much I hated to put on the man-shaped harness and struggle up the towpath, pulling the *Bream* like a beast.

'We could take turns,' I spoke without conviction, but then my heart swelled with the awfulness of selling our keel and I said firmly, 'Bow-hauling's better than going down a mine!'

Mam looked doubtful. 'I've never heard of anyone bow-hauling all the way up from Rotherham. It'd be terrible slow work and back-breaking.'

'But staying here and giving in would be worse,' I insisted.

'Let's do it!' Izzie cried. 'I'm a big lass now, there's plenty my age at work and Jack's too old to be at school.'

'I wanted better for thee, Jack,' Mam whispered. 'That's why we paid the money for school-learning. Whoever heard of a boatman reading and writing fine as thee?'

'That's one thing I wouldn't mind at all,' I laughed. 'I've learnt all they can teach me at that school. I've still got plenty o' time ahead o' me to go and make my fortune.'

'Oh Jack,' Mam got up and kissed me. 'Tha's a good lad.'

'That's it then… settled.' I thumped my fist on the table. 'We cadge a lift up to Rotherham in the morning and hope that we can get there before Father sells the *Silver Bream*!'

'Aye, but…' Mam got up and hurriedly began emptying her stone pots that she kept coins in. 'Money for the rent man, money for the farm lass, money for the milk,' she muttered.

Izzie and I were puzzled. Was she going strange with the worry of it all? We didn't need money to cadge a lift; there were plenty of boatmen who'd take us up the waterway for nothing.

'Nay Mam,' I said. 'What's all these pennies for?'

'There's a better way,' she said. 'A quicker way, if we can just find the fare.'

'What?' we were both puzzled.

'We could go on the evening train from Doncaster and change at Swinton, for Rotherham,' she said. 'Then we could take that load up to Sheffield overnight and get paid in the morning. We could pick up another load by the afternoon and hire a horse!'

'Aye,' I agreed seeing the sense in what she

suggested. 'But – to go on the railway! And how can we get to Doncaster in time?'

'John Adams,' she said, breathless now. 'If we rush up to the Doncaster Road we might just catch John Adams and beg a ride in his carrier's cart.'

I stared at her, amazed.

Mam shrugged her shoulders. 'Those railways haven't done us in yet my lad – and why shouldn't we take advantage of them for once? Your dad might ha' sold the *Bream* by tomorrow, and you know how he swears that a fast 'turn about' is the key to canal work. Time is money! Time is money!' she muttered. 'But – I'm not sure we've enough for the train fares.'

Izzie was suddenly fishing about in her little pouch. 'I've got the money I was saving for my new bonnet!'

'Oh Izzie! Tha's a good lass,' Mam didn't hesitate to take it, and then I knew that I must do the same. I'd been collecting pennies in my spare time, by walking down the towpath to help out at Low Bridge, hoping that I'd eventually have enough for a pair of new boots. None of that mattered now. I could cobble a patch on the toes of my old ones and so I handed my collection of pennies over to mother.

'Thank you,' she said, kissing me. 'I won't forget this. I only hope tha father will think I do right.' She started throwing bread and cheese and apples into a basket. 'We must get going at once, if we're to catch the cart.'

I tried hard to think. 'We'll need extra jackets for bow-hauling,' I said. 'Then at least we'll be warm and padded.'

'Aye, you get them, Jack,' Mam agreed. 'Izzie – fetch some water, love, to put out the fire.'

Suddenly we were rushing about the place in all directions. We sluiced the fire down and barred our shutters, then turned the key in the lock and set off towards the main Doncaster highway. Our cottage had never been left so alone before, but as we strode away laden with coats and baskets, a touch of excitement began to grow inside me. At least we were doing something. This was better than sitting at home waiting and worrying.

Following us down the path came our old cat, mewing loudly.

'Tansy,' cried Izzie. 'What about Tansy?'

'She'll have to see to herself,' Mam said, firmly. 'If all goes well, it won't be long before we're back. She's a grand mouser – she'll not starve.'

'Get away!' I clapped my hands and chased the

cat back towards our small lean-to woodshed. 'There's shelter and mice for you,' I told her.

Tansy settled herself down inside the shed, looking offended, and I ran down the path quickly, before she tried to follow us again.

'Come on,' Mam marched along at a fair lick. 'I can see the cart – we must run!'

4 ❖ The Railway to Rotherham

We arrived at Doncaster Railway Station rather creased and dirty as we'd been sitting on barrels filled with pitch that the carrier was taking on to Rotherham.

'I could take you all the way,' he offered.

'I thank thee kindly,' Mam told him. 'But tha can't get us there as fast as the train, now can tha, John?'

He shook his head and waved to us. The carriers were suffering from the competition of the new railways, just as we were.

The station was bustling; crowds milled about, eating, drinking and wandering around the sacks of post and parcels. It took a while before we could find out where to buy tickets. The money that we'd scraped together was just enough for us to ride third class on the train to Rotherham.

We'd all heard frightening stories about travelling by train, tales of people falling out, exploding engines and people scalded by the steam. Maybe we were risking our lives going like this, even though it was for a good cause. We were herded towards the third class waiting area, away from the food and drink stalls, where a few wealthy travellers were feeding in style.

'Oh Mam, I need the privy,' Izzie whispered.

'Not now, Izzie!' Mam looked even more bothered.

But we looked all around and at last saw that there was a small ladies' room, with a long queue of women all waiting to get in. Then mother saw three coal-pit lasses creeping behind some standing carts piled high with planks of wood. They were beginning to pull up their skirts as they went. 'Tha'll have to go there,' she nodded.

Izzie wasn't very happy at the thought, but she was getting desperate and did as Mam told her. She came back smiling. 'There's plenty o' lasses all doing the same,' she told us.

We didn't have long to wait then before a distant thundering sound made us all look down the track.

'Coming – it's coming!' Everyone picked up baskets and the women tied their bonnets on. The noise grew louder and at last the engine rumbled into sight, great puffs of smoke and steam shooting up from its funnel. As it approached the station it began to slow down, but that seemed to shake the carriages behind all the more, and as it stopped the funnel hissed like a thousand snakes. Though I swore that I'd hate the railways forever, I couldn't stop the bubble of excitement that was growing in my belly. We'd seen and heard the engines before, and I'd always secretly wondered what it would feel like to ride behind one of those steam-belching dragons. I was still angry at what had happened, but I began to think that I might as well enjoy what I could of the ride.

Once the train had stopped, the doors of the third class wagons were thrown open and gangs of swearing navvies swarmed out onto the platform with picks and shovels tied to their packs.

'Watch out!' Mam grabbed Izzie, and pulled her out of their way.

They strode away through the station, shouting instructions to each other as to the whereabouts of the nearest alehouse.

'First class!' the station master called.

The first class travellers began to climb aboard. This was done in a very orderly fashion, with station porters carrying bags, and maids and servants helping their employers to find a seat. Then it was the turn of the second class – those travellers were more noisy and plentiful, and the railway men shouted orders and slammed doors. Then at last the stationmaster bellowed 'third class!' and stood back.

We joined in the mad dash that followed, trying desperately to keep hold of each other. Everyone pushed and shoved and shouted, and we struggled aboard with a gang of dirty-faced pitch workers into the already crowded wagon.

I managed to fight my way to the front and found three empty spaces that I was pleased with. I pulled Mam down beside me.

'Now this is grand,' she said. 'Right at the front, with a fine view.'

My heart was thundering as more steam rose from the engine and a great shrieking hoot came from the driver's cabin. The doors were slammed and a whistle blew, then suddenly great shoots of steam started to burst from the engine, followed by a loud chuff-chuffing sound. The wagons were trembling and we were off.

Izzie grabbed my arm and screamed, then she giggled.

'Hush Izzie!' Mam told her, but she looked scared and excited herself, as the train rattled away.

'Oh help!' I gasped, holding tight to the edge of the seat, as we built up speed.

Faster and faster we went, faster than any cart or carriage, faster than the fastest racehorse, faster than we'd ever gone before in the whole of our lives. We went out through Doncaster, quickly leaving the coalyards and pitch works behind us and on through woods and pastureland, towards Swinton.

The speed of it all was wonderful, but we quickly came to understand why those seats had been free for us to take. The front of the wagon rattled until our teeth ached and a cold current of air blew back into our faces through the open carriage. Our eyes watered, but then all at once it got even worse as a drift of smoke, bearing streams of tiny cinders from the engine funnel, whooshed into our faces. We ducked down, rubbing our eyes, trying to protect ourselves.

'Ah!' Mother growled. 'These seats were not so fine after all!'

The journey seemed to fly by and almost before we'd started we were slowing down and stopping for passengers to get on and off. As three seats behind us became empty, we got up and rushed to claim them, leaving some new passengers to suffer in our place.

As the train pulled away from the station again, it started to rain. Everyone cursed and grumbled and there was a great scramble for scarves and shawls and handkerchiefs as the raindrops came blowing in from the sides. I felt water dripping down my neck, so I pulled out the jackets that I carried, handing them to Izzie and Mam, and pulling the other over my shoulders. One woman emptied out her potatoes and held the sack round her neck, while potatoes rolled about on her lap. Luckily the downpour didn't last too long. We changed trains at Swinton and after a few more stops we arrived in Rotherham, with the setting sun turning our faces pink.

We climbed down from the wagon, with our eyes red and clothes damp, but we'd certainly arrived there very fast. Though we walked on solid ground again, my knees would not stop trembling.

Mam heaved a great sigh of relief. 'Right,' she said. 'Now to find your father, quick as we can, before he sells that boat.'

5 ❖ Who's Captain Now?

We marched along the towpath at Rotherham as the sun began to sink. A few keels moved on steadily up through the River Don, but most were tying up for the night, and the boatmen settling down to get themselves a bite to eat. There were plenty of families here, with small gangs of children playing beside the river and women hanging washing out on lines across the decks or close to the riverbank.

We'd not gone far when we saw the *Silver Bream* tied up in the distance. Father wasn't in the cabin keeping warm and getting himself some food as we'd have expected him to be, but up on deck standing alone at the tiller. His hand stroked the gaily-painted wood as though he was getting ready to steer into a lock, but the *Silver Bream* wasn't going anywhere at all.

Mam stopped for a moment watching him, her face solemn. 'At least the *Bream*'s still there,' she whispered, then set off again along the towpath towards him.

We trotted along behind, struggling to keep up – then Father saw us, and his mouth dropped open in surprise. 'What the devil's thee doing here?' he cried.

'Tha's not sold her yet?' Mam gasped, ignoring his question.

'No,' he shook his head. 'I've not had a chance, and with the mast and leeboards down at Wike Well I'm not sure who'll want to take her on. But – how did thee get here?'

'Never mind that – tha's still got the *Silver Bream* – that's what matters. Now listen here, Alfie, does tha really want to sell her?' she demanded.

Dad stared at her open-mouthed.

'Come on, Alfie – does tha want to sell her?' Mam repeated.

Dad's face crumpled. 'God knows I don't,' he whispered. 'But – what else can I do?' He felt in his pocket and brought out one guinea and a shilling. 'That's all I've got. The price o' poor Jasper's worn out old corpse and a shilling to get us through Tinsley locks.'

'Right!' Mam stepped aboard, ignoring the coins. 'That's all I wanted to know. Tha's got a new crew then, a mate and two helpers! We'll get going at once, and have this grain up at Sheffield by the morning, just you see.'

'No horse!' Dad rubbed his eyes, as though he might be imagining things. He clearly thought that we'd all gone mad.

'Bow-hauling,' I told him, as I jumped aboard. 'That's what we'll do!'

'What? All the way to Sheffield?'

'We can do it, Dad,' Izzie told him. 'See if we can't!'

Then suddenly he was laughing, laughing like a madman and pushing the coins back into his pocket. He wiped a tear from his eye, but still he laughed. 'Now I've heard it all,' he croaked. 'Our Jack offering to bow-haul all the way to Sheffield.' Then he stopped, and said, 'How did tha get here so fast?'

I took a deep breath. 'We came on the railway and we changed our train at Swinton.'

Dad blinked at us in amazement; then he suddenly cracked out laughing again. 'All right,' he said. 'If tha wants to bow-haul to Sheffield, Jack, tha shall!'

And he held out the hated man-harness to me. I gritted my teeth and started to pull it over my head, but suddenly Dad was hugging me, his eyes full of tears again. 'Tha's a son to be proud of,' he said. 'I shall take first turn, lad, but I'll need help later on.

And tha's a wife to be proud of,' he gasped, trying to take Mam into his arms and kiss her.

'No time for that!' She pushed him away. 'Time's money! How many times has tha told me that?' She went over to start unfastening the mooring rope.

'Aye! Aye! All right!' Dad was still shaking his head and smiling, but he picked up the man-harness and slipped it over his shoulders. 'I can see who's captain now.' He stepped ashore and walked up the towpath. 'Give us a bit o' help to get her moving!'

As Mam untied the rope, I ran after Dad and helped him haul on the line as the rope went tight. He tipped his whole body weight steadily forwards and we both leaned into the rope so that the *Silver Bream* gave a little. We did it again and at last our keel started to move. Then with Mam at the tiller and Izzie and me marching up the towpath with windlasses for the locks in our hands, we set off on a journey that just a few hours ago, we'd never have thought to do.

Dad walked on towards Holme Lock and Ickles New Cut. As the first set of gates came into view, we ran ahead to look at the lock.

'Empty!' Izzie shouted.

'That's grand,' Dad puffed. 'At least someone's

on our side.'

I carefully crossed the closed lock gates to the other side of the canal, then Izzie and I both leant on the balance beams to start the lock gates opening. Dad hauled the *Silver Bream* into the lock and once we'd closed the gates behind her, we ran forwards again to fix our windlasses onto the ground paddles and wind them up, letting water flood in.

'Wind steady!' Dad shouted. 'Don't let them snap back in your face!'

But he was too late, and Izzie gave a cry as she faltered, letting the windlass smack back into her cheek.

'Aw lass!' Dad cried.

'I'm fine,' she insisted, quickly catching hold again and setting her paddle winding steadily up.

At last we could watch with satisfaction as the water went pouring in around the *Silver Bream*, gently lifting her up to a higher level. We left the paddles then and went to lean against the balance beams on the top gates, waiting for the sudden give that came when the water was deep enough. We cheered as soon as they started to move and open.

'Never mind cheering!' Mam yelled, as Dad hauled the *Silver Bream* out of the lock. 'Hang on tight to them windlasses, we don't want 'em in the water! Now… on to the next set o' gates.'

When we reached Tinsley Bottom, it was growing dark and by the time we'd worked our way through the first four locks, I was exhausted, with aching arms and shoulders and blistered hands. There were eight more locks to pass through, before we'd have lifted the *Silver Bream* up from the lower water of the river Don, onto the higher level of the Sheffield and Tinsley Canal. Izzie had gone very quiet, stumbling on from one lock gate to the next, her shoulders hunched, rubbing her hands together. Even in the gloom, I could see her cheek burning dark red. I wanted to go and cheer her, but there was no time to spare, we must just march on and on. I couldn't think how Dad was managing to plod steadily on, manhandling the keel through all the tricky gates and I ran back to help him as much as I could.

We couldn't keep going like that all night and as the *Silver Bream* emerged from the fourth lock into a pound of quiet water, Mam called a halt.

'We'll rest,' she announced firmly and I could see that Dad wasn't going to argue with that. 'We'll get moving again at first light.'

We tied up, while Dad went to pay the toll

money, then we went down into our cramped cabin in the fore of the keel and I got a fire going in the stove. Mam served up bread and cheese and a bit of ale.

'Can I have some?' I asked.

Mam poured some ale into a mug for me. 'Do a man's job and you get a man's drink,' she told me.

'What about me?' Izzie asked in a small voice.

'You'll get a woman's drink,' Mam smiled. 'A mug of hot tea.'

6 ❖ A One Guinea Horse

We sat there in the warmth sipping our drinks and before she'd even finished her tea, Izzie had slumped down in the corner, fast asleep. Dad lifted her gently onto one of the smaller bunks and covered her with a rug. We were just about to lie down ourselves when we heard the sound of clopping hooves coming along the towpath. Dad picked up the lantern and climbed the bottom few rungs of the ladder, sticking his head out through the hatch door.

'Johnny Furniss?' We heard him shout. 'What're you up to? That mare's on three legs!'

Dad climbed out and I followed him, as Johnny slowed up beside us and stopped. 'Don't tell me that,' he spoke angrily. 'Blasted mare's been lame for weeks now. I'm taking her down to the knacker's yard.'

Johnny was another keel-owner like Dad, and we often saw him passing up and down the waterway.

'Hang on,' Dad cried. 'Hold up this lantern,

Jack! Let's have a look at her.'

We heard Mam huffing behind us. The last thing she wanted was Dad getting involved with other folks' horses, when we'd not even got one of our own. But Dad was already off the keel and examining the grey mare's painful leg. I jumped ashore and took the lantern, holding it high. As I stood there I ran my hand along the mare's body, she was so thin that you could feel her ribs, and though I still couldn't see very much, I felt the roughness of deep sores on her shoulders. I said nothing, for I knew that some canal folk stopped feeding or caring once they'd decided that a horse was headed for the knacker's yard. It was something my father would never do, but it just wasn't done to pass comment.

'Come round here,' Dad told me, 'and bring that light down a bit.'

As I went to stand beside her head, the mare snorted and turned, nuzzling desperately at my pocket for a tit-bit, while she patiently let Dad pull up her front left hoof. I wished that I'd got something for her.

Dad bent and sniffed at the hoof. 'Wet rot!' he said. 'Give us a bit o' time and I could cure that for you, Johnny.'

'Time's what I've not got!' Johnny told him. 'I've a load o' coals stuck up beyond T'acky Dock and another horse hired and ready at Bottom Lock. This beggar's just no good t' me.'

The rough nose nuzzled again and blew warm horse-breath into my hand. I missed our old Jasper at that moment and I felt very sorry for this poor beast. 'Could we take her?' I asked.

I knew it was a stupid thing to suggest, when all the money that my dad had got was the one guinea that he'd been paid for Jasper's worn-out corpse.

'Eh dear!' Mam sighed. 'If that mare's no good to Johnny, I'm sure it's no good to us!' she muttered.

But Dad had heard what I said and he fished in his pocket and brought out the one guinea. 'Now that's all I've got,' he said. 'Mind you Johnny – the knacker will give thee no more than that. Let me have thy mare and save theesen a journey for nowt.'

'Well now…' Johnny hesitated. He looked from me to Dad, then shook his head and laughed. 'Tha's a mad fellow, Alfie North, and this lad o' yours is just as daft, but if tha really wants the nag – have her.' He took the coin and handed me the leading rein. 'Best o' luck to thee!' he called as he went striding fast away, down towards Bottom Lock.

Mam stood on the deck with folded arms. 'He's

right – tha's mad, Alfie North.' She gave my arm a punch then, 'and tha's barmy too, our Jack!'

But Father was wide awake and excited now. 'Now then, lass,' he soothed. 'We've done very well to get so far – very well indeed. I swear I can get this nag sorted and then we'll have got ourselves a new horse for just one guinea. Fetch us Jasper's tools, our Jack.'

'Humph!' Mam huffed. 'A lame, one guinea horse; that'll get us far.'

'Let him try,' I begged, as I came back from the cabin with the box of horse medication and hoof cutting tools. 'A decent meal is what it really needs,' I said, looking hopefully at Mam. 'Its ribs stick out like ladders.'

I didn't think it the moment to mention the sores as well.

'Humph!' she said again, but she went back in the cabin and fetched a pan, then she went and took a good scoop of grain from our boatload, and set about boiling it up. I held up the lantern, while Father levered off the worn, jagged horseshoe and started cutting a lot of bad-smelling stuff away from the hoof. The mare backed away in panic and kicked my shin hard.

Father spoke soothing words, calling the mare

his 'little love' and 'sweetheart', ignoring the string of swear words that poured from my lips. 'Should a' let Johnny Furniss walk on,' I growled.

When the boiled mash was cooled a bit, Mam filled Jasper's nosebag, and slipped it over the grey mare's head. The horse ate greedily while Dad still worked at the hoof, and the mash seemed to settle her down and make her easier to deal with. I rubbed my shin, and tried to be forgiving.

'She's not been fed for days,' Mam said, a touch of disapproval at Johnny's treatment of the mare creeping into her voice.

'Will tha boil up some Stockholm tar?' Father asked.

'I might!' said Mam grudgingly, but she went back to the cabin and did as he asked.

'Her shoulders are bad too,' I told Dad in a low voice.

'Aye,' Dad sighed. He brought out the fuller's earth and gently began to treat the sores.

Mam came back with a steaming pot of the strong-smelling tar, and held it while Dad painted the inside of the hoof.

'Don't tha trample me again,' I muttered. The mare flicked her ears and stayed calm, munching steadily away at her mash.

When he'd done all he could, Dad rummaged about in his box of horse-gear and brought out a soft leather shoe that he'd sometimes used for Jasper. He fitted it over the treated hoof and we all stood back, hoping to see the mare put her hoof to the ground, but she still held it raised a little.

'Well – we shall just have to wait and see,' Dad said. 'When we get to Attercliffe I shall get Robert Awdas to take a look at her. He's the best smith on the canal and I know he'll wait for payment till we're coming back. Tether her will you, Jack? We must all get some sleep now.'

7 ✤ Neep's Luck

My mind was still whirling when I settled down on the narrow bunk, with Mam and Dad already gently snoring in the double fold-down bed at my feet. I thought I'd never get to sleep, so much had happened in the space of one day, but exhaustion took over and I slept at last. The next thing I heard was Mam rustling about in the cabin, opening and shutting cupboard doors, and setting the kettle to boil. When I pulled aside the curtain, the first fingers of light were lifting the darkness.

'We'd best be under way,' Mam said when she noticed me awake. 'Can't waste a moment o' daylight.'

Out on the bank-side I saw a sight that pleased me greatly. 'That horse is on four legs,' I cried.

'Eh, what?' Dad sat up in his bunk, fully dressed and immediately wide-awake. He swung his legs down and scrambled straight up the ladder.

Izzie woke up yawning. Her cheek had turned blue, but she didn't seem bothered by it. 'Where are we…?' she murmured.

'We're on the *Silver Bream*,' I reminded her. 'Come outside and see what we've got.'

'A horse – we've got a horse!' Izzie cried, when she saw the grey mare. 'The Neeps have brought her in the night.'

Mam and me laughed at that, thinking Johnny Furniss very far from being a water sprite. We watched from the keel as Dad walked the mare up and down. There was a definite improvement; the horse put her hoof to the ground, but still hobbled a little as she walked.

'I said Neeps were lucky,' Izzie insisted. 'Can we call this horse Neep?'

Mam chuckled. 'Aye – if you must. We need a bit o' fairy's luck I think. Will you try her on the line Alfie?'

Dad shook his head. 'She's not ready yet. Another good mash might help and some more fuller's earth, then sick horse or not, we must all move on.'

So we set off again, and I had to open and close most of the lock gates myself, as Izzie lead the newly-christened Neep along.

Though we'd started very early, it took most of the morning to work our way up through the rest of the Tinsley Flight of locks. By noon I felt as though

I'd done a whole day's work. My legs and feet ached and my hands were raw.

Once we'd come out of the Top Lock into the canal, Mam and I took over bow-hauling, with a harness each, but marching along together. At least I could give my hands a rest, though my back and shoulders must now take the strain. We passed the small coal wharves as we travelled on towards Attercliffe and the long chimney stack of the famous Huntsman Works, where they'd made the first fine steel in crucible pots.

I plodded along beside Mam, trying to walk in step with her. We dare not stop, for if we did, we'd have the extra hard job of getting the boat moving again. It was best to keep going slow and steady and I thought sadly of our old Jasper, and how he'd patiently pulled the *Silver Bream* for most of his life.

It was back-breaking work, and when Izzie came up behind us, telling us that Dad said to stop, so he'd take over, I was ready to do as she said.

But Mam had a different idea, or so it seemed. 'We'll just get to T'acky Dock!' she insisted. 'Tell him that's where we'll stop.'

So we struggled on under Broughton Lane Bridge. 'Is this the place where Spencer was hanged?' I asked.

'Aye,' Mam shuddered and nodded. 'Terrible, terrible!' she said. 'Just a bit further up, at the crossroads on Attercliffe Common.'

'I'm glad we didn't pass here late last night,' I said.

'Me too,' she whispered.

Mam had often told us the fearful story of Spencer Broughton, who'd robbed the Rotherham mail. He'd been captured and hanged at York, but that wasn't the end of the story. Spencer's body had been sent back to Attercliffe and hanged on a gibbet in chains to warn others against the serious offence of highway robbery. His remains had still been hanging there when Mam was a little girl; she'd seen them just once, and never forgotten. 'Ooh, I can't tell you what nightmares it gave me,' she'd say.

We didn't speak much after that, for it seemed a waste of energy and we needed all we'd got just to keep our keel moving. 'T'acky Dock' was our name for the stone-built aqueduct that carried the canal high above the turnpike road, and I was relieved when at last it came into sight.

'Tie her up,' Dad shouted.

At last Mam stopped and let the lines go slack. 'Aye,' she whispered. 'I don't know about thee,

Jack, but I'm done in!'

'Come on,' I told her, pulling the harness over her head. 'Get theesen some rest, Mam; get into that warm cabin for a bit.'

Mam fretted as we shared a mug of ale. 'We've lost enough time,' she muttered. 'What with that useless horse an' all and now tha father wants to stop at Attercliffe!'

I stuck my head out of the hatch, so that I could see the grassy canal bank-side where we'd tethered the horse. 'She's still on four legs and cropping grass with a will,' I said.

'She'll be better still for a bit of attention from Robert,' Dad insisted.

So we set off again, with Dad and me bow-hauling and Mam at the tiller, until we reached Robert Awdas's smithy.

Robert whistled through his teeth when he saw the state of our poor mare. 'Neep, is it?' Robert laughed. 'Well this beast needs a bit of Neep's Luck, that's for sure!'

We ate bread and cheese while Robert shaped a new horseshoe and I think we all felt better for some food. When Robert had finished his work the Neep seemed to be walking well.

'Try her on the line!' Mam insisted. 'See if she'll earn her keep!'

'Aye, all right,' Dad agreed at last.

So Izzie scrambled back round to the stern of the keel and brought out Jasper's old harness and hauling line. Dad fastened it onto the skinny horse, with Izzie clucking and soothing and patting her neck, while I dropped a pit prop that we kept for the purpose into the lutchet that held up our mast and sails.

I fastened the horse line to it. 'Ready now!' I shouted.

'Now we'll see!' Mam stood back looking doubtful, as Dad led the mare up the towpath, until the line grew taut.

We all held our breath as she stopped, feeling the heavy weight of the keel behind her. 'Now then lass, come on then lass, come on now me sweetheart,' Dad chirruped and slowly she leaned into the rope, throwing her weight forwards, wiry muscles straining with effort, until the boat gave a bit.

'Tha's a grand lass!' Dad spoke soft and encouraging. 'Tha's grand!'

The Neep leaned again and suddenly the boat was moving; she was off, clopping steadily up the towpath on all four hooves, dragging the *Silver*

Bream behind her.

'She were born to it!' Dad shouted, his face pink and joyful as he strode along to catch her up. 'Born to it! Sheffield here we come! Grab the tiller, Jack!'

We cheered and Mam and Izzie had to run fast to catch up and jump aboard.

8 ❖ To Sheffield and Back

We went at a good pace through the great open expanse of Attercliffe Cut, where Old Tommy and so many of the unemployed had worked, thirty years ago, to build the canal. We passed through the wide pool that we call the 'winding hole', as it's the only place wide enough for boats to turn around in.

'Well, I take back all I said,' Mam said, as the Neep walked on. 'That horse must be blessed by the water fairies after all!'

Mam took the tiller and I went to join Dad for a bit. He was in good spirits now, but as I went to walk beside him, he smiled a little sadly. 'I never wanted this for my family,' he said. 'I wanted a better life for thee, Jack.'

'But Dad,' I told him, my voice low with feeling, 'I'm happy. For all me battered shins and sore hands, I wouldn't want to go back to school. We're all working together; I'm right enjoying messen.'

He smiled again, but he shook his head. 'Tha'll not be so jolly when we start coming back through the Needle's Eye.'

The little workshops of Attercliffe were left behind us and ahead of us the canal banks grew thick with great barn-like work sheds. These new steelworks had been set up in recent years, and now the skyline towards Sheffield was marked with their chimney-stacks, belching out thick smoke. Grey steel-dust and wheel-swarf seemed to cover everything: the grass, the sheds, the stacked iron bars and even the men who worked there.

'It starts to get mucky here,' I murmured.

'Oh aye, it does,' Dad agreed. 'Old Benjamin Huntsman didn't know what he were starting. Every time I come up to t' Basin, another work-shed and chimney's appeared. Now this here's George Marriot's Steel-Works, he's a bit of a toff by all accounts. His workmen swear that he wears these new, long straight trousers, instead o' proper breeches like most of us.'

'How does he bend his knees?' I asked.

'I'm sure I don't know,' Dad was happy now, and talkative. 'Britches wi' chimney pipes on 'em, that's what they say.'

One of the men working at Marriot's Wharfe called out to Dad. 'I see tha's lost a horse an' found one, Alfie North!'

'Aye, I have,' Dad replied. 'I lost a crew and got

another too!'

'There's plenty o' bagged and finished hand tools to be shifted from here for the Humber,' he called.

'Right,' Dad agreed. 'I'll see thee in the morning.'

Then in the distance ahead of us, we saw Bacon Lane Bridge coming up; the Needle's Eye.

'Right,' said Dad, slowing the horse down. 'Now we have to go a bit careful through here, but it's coming back with an empty boat that's the real trouble.'

The Neep ducked her head and walked on underneath the bridge, just changing her direction a little so that the line didn't catch on the awkward angle of the bridge.

'That mare could take a keel up to Sheffield all by herself,' Dad swore.

Dad went back to the tiller and Izzie came to walk beside me, encouraging the Neep with sweet words and gentle pats.

'Now that'll be a good clean load to pick up,' I told her. 'Finished hand tools from Marriot's, all bagged up and neat. There'll be no gritty coal dust to sweep out when we get to Hull, ready for more grain.'

'Eh Jack – tha sounds just like tha father. Tha

sounds like a proper keelman already.'

I was well pleased with that. 'One day I'll run the *Silver Bream* myself,' I told her. 'And tha'll be mate, if tha likes.'

'Aye. I will,' she said, smiling and gently touching her bruised cheek.

We passed under Cadman Street Bridge and into the wide canal basin. A great spreading mass of steel works and blast furnaces surrounded the waterside and our heads turned this way and that, for it was a wild sight. Huge sprays of sparks shot up into the air, as our ears grew used to the constant clang of hammers. Every now and then a fierce fizzing sound would come from the open work-sheds, as they cooled bars of red-hot iron in water.

'Are there queues ahead?' Izzie shaded her eyes to see.

'It's not too bad.' I smiled. 'We'll have delivered by dusk, then maybe we'll get a bit of a rest.'

The Neep clopped obediently over the swing bridge, and we released the line and told Izzie to hold the bridle. 'Well done, lass!' I gave the mare a quick scratch behind the ears. A sore shin was small price to pay for such a grand horse.

'Aye – your water sprites have done us proud,'

said Dad.

Mam stepped off the *Silver Bream*, nodding her head in agreement. 'I say when I'm wrong – and I were wrong about that horse. She's grand – and I've filled another nosebag with mash for her!'

Izzie stroked the grey nose. 'She deserves a feast,' she said.

Then Dad took the tiller, while Mam and me hauled on the line, pulling the fore of the keel round to the 'boat hole' that was built into the bottom of the terminal warehouse. This was another tricky bit, but Dad was skilled at the tiller and he soon had the *Bream* nosing her way neatly inside. The boat fitted perfectly into the stone-built hole and while Dad and the warehouse workers dug out the cargo of grain, we fed the Neep.

'We heard tha were in trouble, Alfie North,' the warehouse men said.

'We heard tha were ready to pack it in!'

'I damn near did,' Dad told them, but then he nodded his head at us, with a touch of pride. 'But I were not allowed! I'm off back down to the Humber wi' the missus and young 'uns. We'll pick up bagged tools from Marriot's.'

'That's grand!' They gave us a bit of

encouragement.

Dad was grinning now. 'I found mesen a one-guinea horse,' he said. 'And our little lass is determined to call it the Neep.'

'Neep's luck is what you've got!' they all agreed. 'Will you take on ballast?'

'I shall have to think,' said Dad.

The cargo of grain was delivered as the light began to fade.

'Let's turn about,' said Mam, when the hold was empty again. 'We could get down to the Needle's Eye before it gets really dark. Then we'd be well on our way.'

Dad shook his head. 'But without taking iron bars aboard to give us weight, we'll not get through the Needle's Eye too easy.'

We groaned at the thought of taking on iron just to get us under the bridge, and having to heave it all off again before we could take our new cargo aboard.

All the canal-folk grumbled about the way that Bacon Lane Bridge had been built very low, to carry the road over the canal. When a keel was heavy-laden it would pass through the Needle's Eye without too much trouble, but when it was empty and riding high in the water, it could be very difficult to get through.

But then again, loading up with iron bars wasted so much time.

'I'm for risking it,' said Mam. 'Time is money! That's what I've been told so often. I can't do with all this loading on and off!'

Dad laughed and kissed her nose. 'Aye, aye! Captain!' he agreed. 'Have it thy way!'

So we moved on, out of the busy canal basin and tied up in a quieter space, on the Sheffield side of the Needle's Eye, where the Neep could crop a bit of grass while we slept.

9 ❖ The Needle's Eye

Dad woke us early next morning, anxious to get under way. As soon as we'd swigged a bit of tea we all came up on deck, ready to tackle the bridge. Mam and Izzie took up poles and stepped onto the towpath; I took a crowbar from the deck. Dad fastened the Neep to the line and the horse walked steadily under the bridge, but then stopped and turned to wait. I swear she knew we were in for trouble.

'Right – get her nose through first,' said Mam.

'Hang about,' said Dad, beginning to haul on the line. 'I'm in charge.'

I stared at the bridge and at our solid keel riding high in the water; it just didn't look as though it was possible for it to get through. There was no wonder they called it the Needle's Eye. 'Perhaps we should have gone for ballast,' I said.

'Hush up,' Mam hissed. 'Just get its nose under!'

For a moment as Dad hauled the keel forward, it looked as though we just might be lucky, but then with a nasty grinding scraping sound, the *Silver*

Bream stuck firmly, half-way through the Needle's Eye.

'Damn it!' Dad growled at Mam. 'Tha wouldn't let me take on iron bars!'

'Me?' Mam spat back at him. 'I never forced thee, I just gave advice. Tha's in charge, Alfie North!'

Dad just shook his head.

Mam dug her pole into the ground and stood there, hands on hips. 'Well – I've a good mind to get on that train and go home again, if this is all the thanks I get!'

Izzie went to hold the Neep's bridle, looking worried. She hid her face in the mare's rough mane, stroking and soothing, though I don't think there was any danger of the horse going off ahead, with the *Bream* stuck fast.

Dad hauled again and manoeuvred, while I clambered up onto the bridge, and hung over the side, leaning out with my crowbar, trying to ease the boat through, where it was sticking.

'Damn and blast it!' Dad swore.

'I'll not have that language, Alfie North!' Mam was red in the face now and trying hard again to push the boat through with her pole.

While we struggled there, a grain-loaded keel appeared, going in the other direction, towards

Sheffield. It was the *Good Maud,* one of the Stainforth family-run boats, its deck full of children.

'That's all we need,' Mam muttered, her face running with sweat. 'Now we're blocking up the way as well! It'd be easier to take the damned thing out o' the water and carry it round the blasted bridge!'

'Oooh, language!' Dad whistled through his teeth.

Next thing I knew, Mam gave her pole a great shove and lost it along with her balance. There was an enormous splash and suddenly she was in the canal, spouting dirty water.

'Mammy!' Izzie screamed.

Dad dropped the line and ran to Mam, managing to grab hold of her strong apron strings. I raced down from the bridge and snatched hold of one flailing hand. Mam gasped and spouted more water. She felt very heavy with her skirts all waterlogged and I couldn't see how we were going to heave her out. But then I looked up at the sound of clattering feet and saw that the family from the *Good Maud* were off their keel and running fast across the bridge towards us.

Mam was hauled out of the canal by many hands.

She streamed with water, tears of distress and shame adding to the flow. 'I've brought nowt wi' me!' she cried. 'I'm half drowned and nowt to change into!'

'Here, lass!' The woman from the *Good Maud* took her arm. 'Come wi' me. I've a petticoat and shawl you can borrow. Come wi' me back to the *Good Maud* and we'll get thee dried.'

'But we're stuck,' Mam sobbed. 'Stuck in the Needle's Eye!'

'Oh, my lot can sort that out,' the woman soothed. 'You leave it to them!'

We watched as the woman led Mam away over the bridge and I wondered how on earth these hordes of children could sort out our problem. But then without a 'by your leave,' they all turned and trooped aboard the *Silver Bream*. Ducking their heads down, beneath the stone span of the bridge, they crept down to the fore deck. Suddenly I understood – there were so many of them, that they amounted to quite a bit of weight and Izzie followed them aboard to add her bit too.

I ran back up onto the bridge with my crowbar and the man went to help Dad hauling on the line, both of them cursing the fellow who built the bridge, whoever he was.

'Damned fool!' Dad muttered.

'Knew nowt of canal work!' the other man growled.

They heaved on the line, while I hung over the bridge, digging down with my crowbar, trying to release the sticking point. I don't know whether it was that or the extra weight of the children, but when they heaved again, the keel at last gave a grinding sound and moved on through, just juddering a bit as she went.

Mam came away from the *Good Maud* in worn, dry clothes, her face bright with relief. 'Bless 'em,' she cried. 'They've got her through! I thought we'd be here all morning! Oh, I can't thank you all enough, I can't!' Then her eyes were full of tears again.

'You'll maybe do the same for me one of these days,' the woman smiled, as her many children trooped back aboard the *Good Maud*.

The Neep waited patiently, while we got ourselves back on board the *Silver Bream* again, then walked steadily on towards Marriot's Wharfe, stopping as soon as Dad cried 'Whoa!'

We loaded up again with bags of hand tools, then carried on and slogged our way without a break through the flight of Tinsley Locks.

As we moved on out into the River Don, Izzie asked 'Where now?'

Her bruised face was pale and smudged with dust – she looked such a sight.

'We'll try and get down to Kilnhurst tonight,' Dad told her. 'Then with a bit o' luck and this fine mare of ours, tomorrow night we'll stop at home.'

'Home,' I murmured. I'd been keen enough to get away from the cottage, but the thought of a comfortable night sounded like bliss to me now.

We went on through Rotherham and reached Kilnhurst before it was dark, mooring up close to where other families had stopped. We slept soundly, with the Neep tethered up on the bank side, but were moving again at first light. We went down to the horse ferry, where the towpath changed sides and a flat chain-drawn barge carried horses over to the other side.

We all watched anxiously as Dad led the Neep aboard the ferry. Some horses didn't like this one little bit and would stamp and fret, and sometimes they'd panic and end up in the water. Quite a few horses had been lost that way.

'Hush, girl, hush!' Dad soothed.

'Aye, hush up,' Mam said. 'I couldn't bear to lose this grand little mare now.'

But we needn't have worried. The Neep took the horse-ferry in her stride, just as she'd done all the other obstacles of the waterway, and we were soon off again towards Swinton.

As we came out of Sprotbrough Lock, there was a long queue of keels and sloops all waiting to come up through the gates, and who should we pass but Johnny Furniss? He was waiting there with his mate and his hired horse.

We couldn't stop the huge grins that came to our faces as Johnny watched the Neep clopping steadily along, pulling the *Silver Bream* as if she'd done it all her life. He stared open-mouthed and Dad waved cheerfully at him.

'Now then, Johnny!' he cried.

'Well tha certainly got the best o' that bargain, Alfie North,' he shouted.

'Aye,' said Mam, wagging a finger at him. 'And there's no going back!'

Johnny was still there gawping after us as we vanished into the lovely, flower-filled woodland that we passed on our way to Swinton.

We travelled on through Doncaster and Stainforth, where the towpath changed to the other side again. We had to unhitch the Neep and lead her over the bridge, where boatyards and ropeworks had recently sprung up at the side of the canal. Both Mam and Dad had been determined to get us home and we arrived just as it was growing dark. Our old cat came trotting up the towpath to meet us, making a terrible noise, complaining at being left behind.

'Oh, poor little Tansy,' Izzie crooned and yawned. 'Were tha left all alone?'

It felt grand to lead the Neep into our tiny paddock, with its own warm stable in the corner.

'Jasper wouldn't mind, would he?' Izzie said, blinking back tears.

'No,' I agreed. 'He'd never have minded sharing with a hard-working mare like the Neep.'

It was bliss to be back in our own beds and next morning Mam let us sleep in a bit, but by noon we were off again, heading down the Stainforth to Keadby canal. But as soon as Mam and Izzie had stepped aboard, our cat came howling along the towpath after us.

'We've not got time to stop,' Mam warned, as she saw the concern on Izzie's face.

'I'm not leaving her again,' Izzie protested, suddenly threatening to leap ashore. 'I'll stay behind with her myself! I'm not leaving Tansy.' She broke into wild sobbing.

Dad and I just ignored her and set off, walking

up the towpath beside the Neep.

'Stop that noise,' Mam told Izzie sharply. 'Stop that noise, lady, and I'll see what I can do!'

Izzie stopped at once then puzzled, while Mam clicked her fingers and gave her special feeding call. 'Puss, puss, puss! Here pussy-puss!'

The next thing we knew, Tansy had jumped aboard the *Silver Bream* and was rubbing round Mam's ankles as she stood at the tiller.

'Now then, does that please thee, lady?' Mam asked.

'Yes it does!' Izzie dashed away her tears.

'Give her a drop o' milk, that'll settle her down - and hush up all that noise!'

Dad and I laughed. 'Now that's all of us aboard,' I said.

10 ◈ Epilogue

The Neep hauled us down to Wike Well Bridge to pick up our mast and leeboards, for any good keel-man loves to sail whenever the deeper water and winds will allow it. There were plenty of boats moored in the canal, so that the boatmen and their families could have a rest at home, and get their boats smart and fettled, with fresh coats of paint and newly waterproofed tarpaulins; but there was no resting up for us.

Dad left the Neep grazing in a field, close to Wike Well Bridge. He had an arrangement with the farmer, who scratched his head in surprise when he saw our new mare.

'Tha's done very well for theesen,' was the farmer's verdict, when he heard the sad tale of Jasper.

We fixed the mast into the lutchet and raised our two square sails.

'Our Jack is getting his wish,' said Izzie. 'To sail right down to the sea.'

'Not quite that far,' Dad laughed.

We moored up for the night once we were past Keadby and had a good rest while we waited for the flood tide and a good wind.

Dad woke us early next morning. 'Come on,' he said. 'There's a fine keelman's breeze blowing and we mustn't waste it.'

So early next morning we sailed down the east side of the Trent and out into the wide River Humber. Our hair blew wildly about our faces and our lungs were filled with fresh salty air.

Izzie laughed with excitement. 'Look at Tansy!' she cried.

The cat had made herself at home aboard the *Silver Bream*, scampering all over the deck, sniffing excitedly at every corner. She now emerged from the hatch with something in her mouth. 'She's caught a rat! She's caught a rat!' Izzie shrieked.

Mam smiled, I hadn't seen her looking so happy for a long time. She went to stand close to Dad. 'We should 'a done this years ago Alfie!' she said.

Dad put his arm about her. 'Here, take the tiller, Jack,' he told me. 'Take the tiller and keep her steady – just a little to the right, there's a good south-westerly and she don't need much help. We'll be in Hull in no time at this rate.'

And so, with my heart in my mouth I took the

tiller and steered the *Silver Bream* out into the great grey expanse of water and sky.

Glossary

Aft   The back of a boat

Ballast   Material taken aboard to add weight

Bow-hauling When a person pulls the keel along rather than a horse

Cut   The canal

Fettled   Repaired

Fore   The front of a boat

Fuller's earth A type of clay used as an absorbent

Gibbet   An upright post with an arm on which the bodies of executed criminals were left hanging as a warning to others

Keel   A flat-bottomed barge, used for navigation of North-Eastern waterways. The name is of Norse origin.

It usually had two square-rigged sails (main sail and topsail)

Leeboards   Plank fixed to the side of a flat-bottomed boat and let down into the water to stop the boat drifting downwind

Lutchet   A box-like timber holder that held the mast. When the mast was removed, a pit prop would be dropped in it to fasten the hauling rope to

Wharf   A level quayside area to which a ship may be moored to load and unload

Windlass   A handle, used to wind lock paddles up or down

Wheel-swarf   Metallic dust, the residue from metalwork on a grinding wheel

Further Reading

Fiction

Jill Paton Walsh – *The Butty Boy*, Puffin
Mary John – *A Shilling for the Gate*, Gomer Press
Geoffrey Trease – *No Horn at Midnight*,
 Macmillan
Marjorie Dunn – *The Maggie Kelly*, The
 Hallamshire Press

Non-fiction

Mike Taylor – *The River Don in old picture
postcards*, Reflections of a Bygone Age
Mike Taylor – *The Sheffield and South Yorkshire
 Navigation*, Tempus Publishing
John Guy – *Victorian Life*, Ticktock Publishing
Simon Ogden – *The Sheffield and Tinsley Canal*,
 The Hallamshire Press

http://www.mike-stevens.co.uk
This is a good website, both informative and fun,
with canal history pages, reviews of books on
canals, and pictures and advice about keeping cats
on canal boats!